TIME
CAPSULE

TIME CAPSULE

LAUREN REDNISS

MAKE ME A WORLD
New York

MAKE ME A WORLD is an imprint dedicated to exploring the vast possibilities of contemporary childhood. We strive to imagine a universe in which no young person is invisible, in which no kid's story is erased, in which no glass ceiling presses down on the dreams of a child. Then we publish books for that world, where kids ask hard questions and we struggle with them together, where dreams stretch from eons ago into the future and we do our best to provide road maps to where these young folks want to be. We make books where the children of today can see themselves and each other. When presented with fences, with borders, with limits, with all the kinds of chains that hobble imaginations and hearts, we proudly say — no.

Visit us on the Web! rhcbooks.com

Educators and librarians, for a variety of teaching tools, visit us at RHTeachersLibrarians.com

Library of Congress Cataloging-in-Publication Data is available upon request.

ISBN 978-0-593-42593-0 (trade) | ISBN 978-0-593-42594-7 (lib. bdg.) | ISBN 978-0-593-42595-4 (ebook)

The text of this book is set in 20-point Eusapia LR, a typeface designed by Lauren Redniss.

The images were created with mixed media.

Book design by Lauren Redniss

MANUFACTURED IN CHINA

April 2022

10 9 8 7 6 5 4 3 2 1

First Edition

First,

she found an empty jar.

Then,

she cut out the date from the newspaper

and glued it to the bottom of the jar.

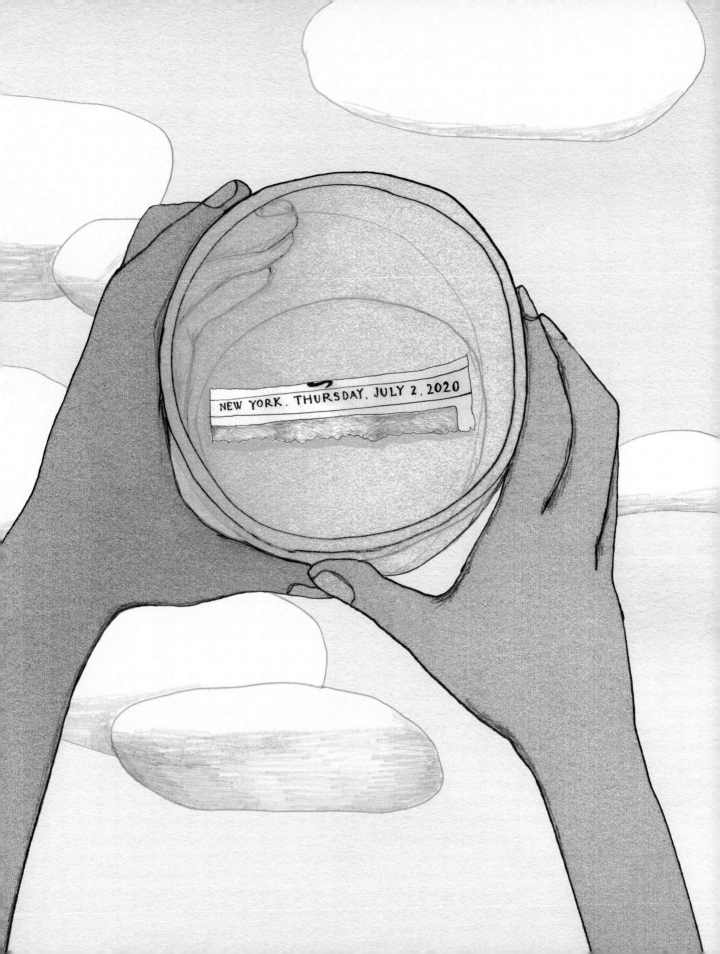

Next,

she put in a pair of lucky dice.

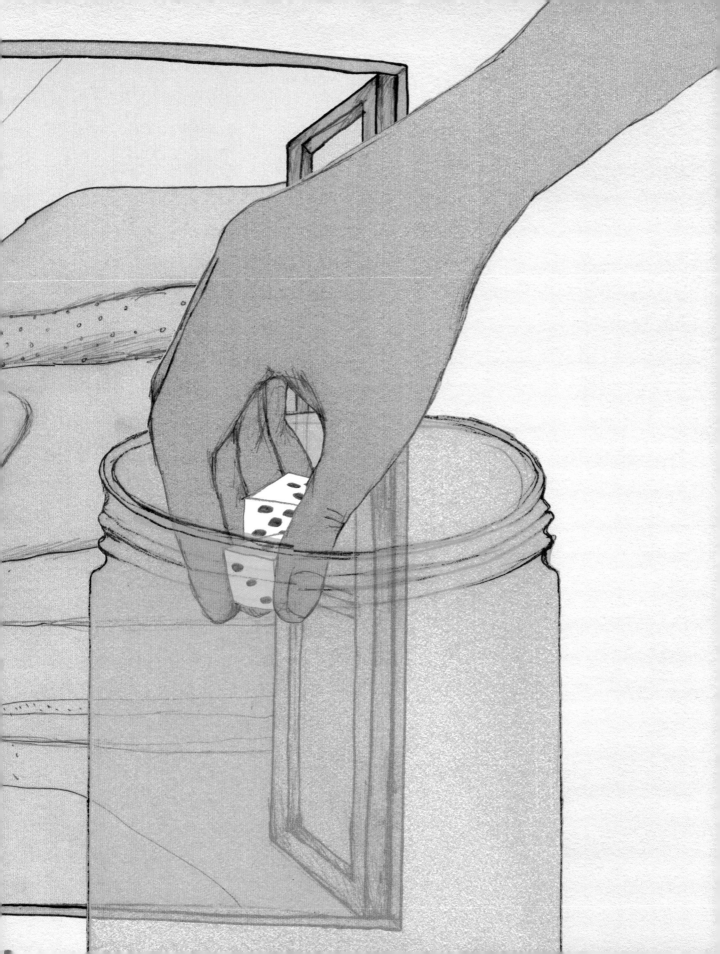

She added her tooth,

which had fallen out a week earlier.

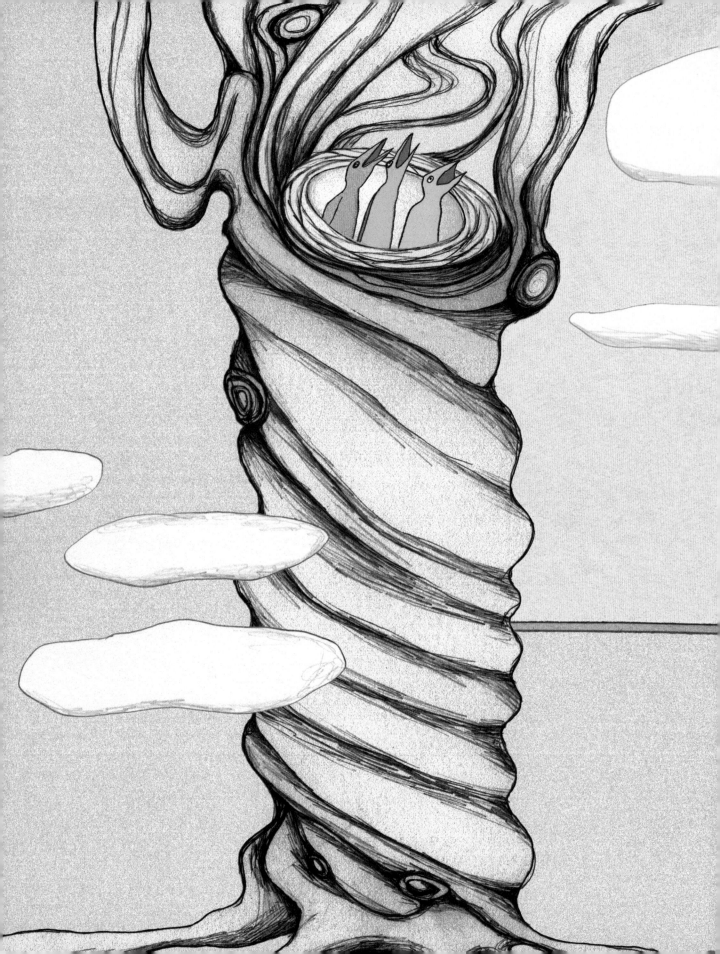

She added an acorn from her favorite tree.

The ring her grandmother had given her.

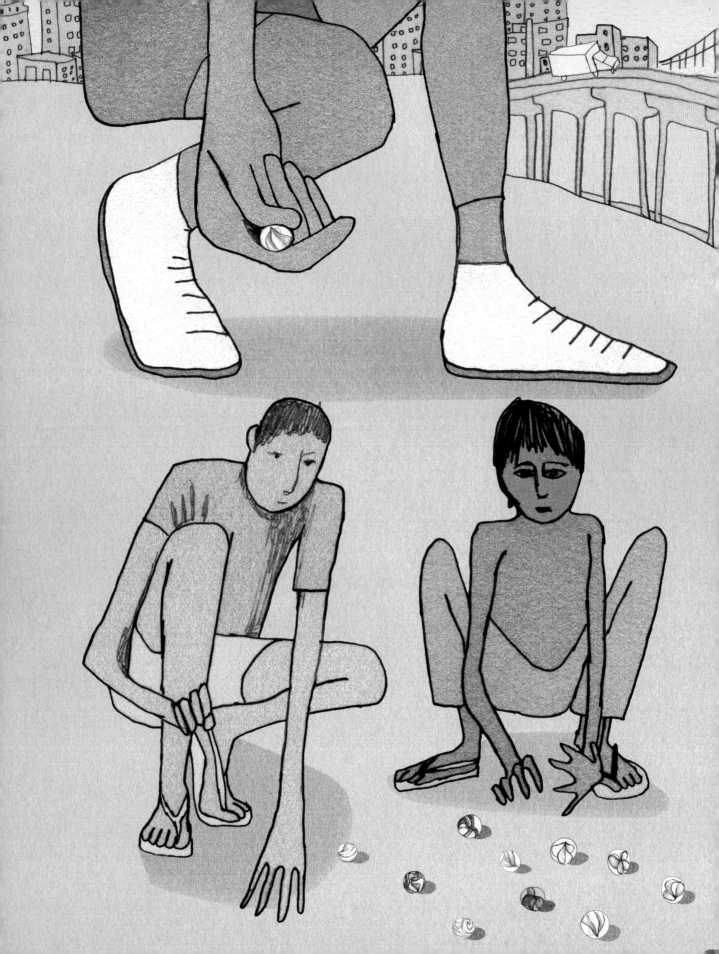

A blue marble.

A plastic sheep named Walter.

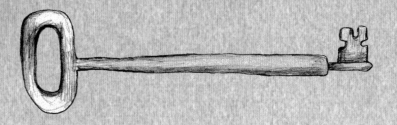

The key to an old house.

The ticket from a visit to the aquarium.

She added a nightmare about a terrible storm.

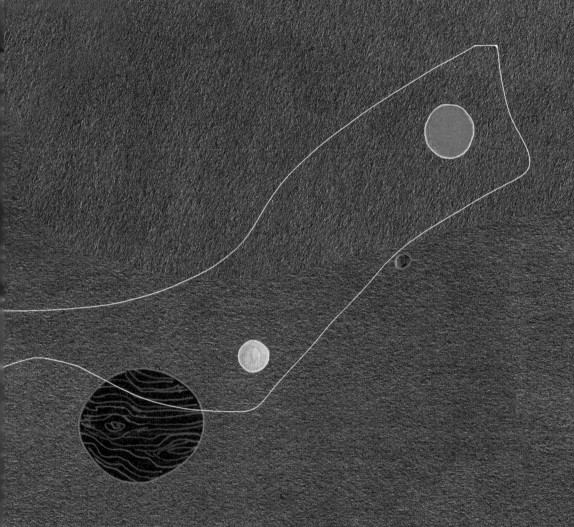

And her dream about outer space.

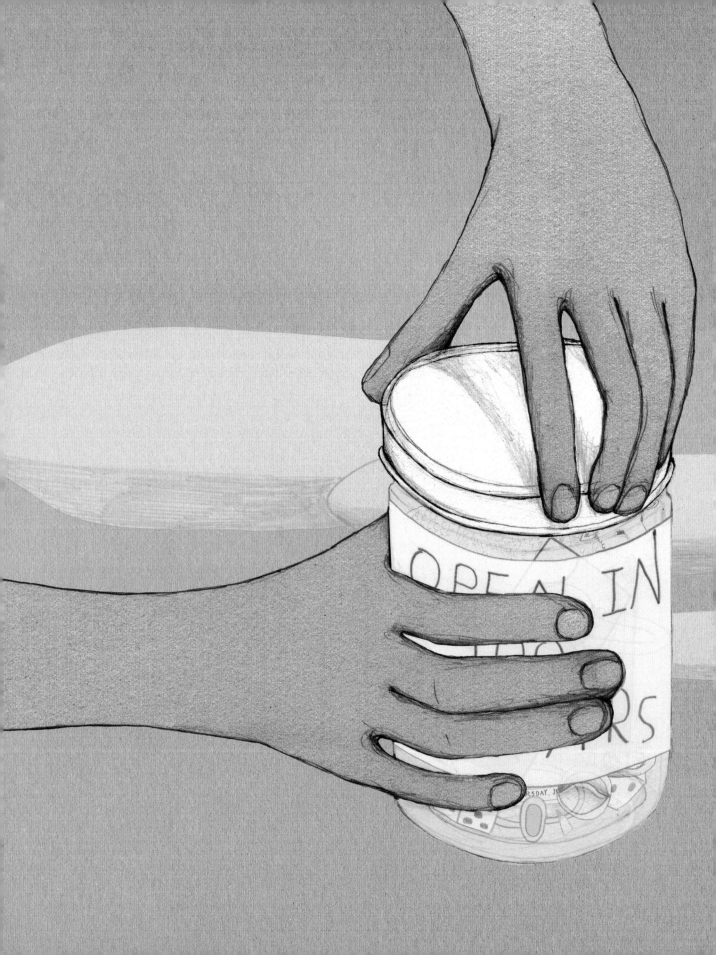

She sealed the jar.

She buried it,

and wondered,

Who,

in the future,

would find her

time capsule?

AUTHOR'S NOTE

I. The World's First "Time Capsule"

It was just before noon on September 23, 1938, at the site of the World's Fair in Queens, New York. The sound of a bronze gong reverberated through the air. A crowd gathered, and in a gesture of reverence, the men removed their hats. A seven-and-a-half-foot-long torpedo-shaped object on a heavy chain was lowered slowly into a hole deep in the earth.

In the 1938 ceremony, the Westinghouse Electric & Manufacturing Company made history. Over the previous

summer, G. Edward Pendray, an advisor to the company, had an idea to drum up publicity. He suggested that Westinghouse bury a container stuffed with archival materials to be retrieved by "futurians" in the year 6939. Pendray

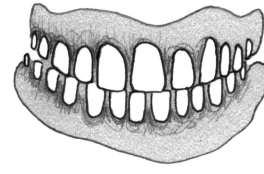

initially called his idea a "time bomb." Later he revised the name to time capsule, thus coining a term that would become ubiquitous in popular culture, both as a way to describe artifacts hidden away for rediscovery at some future date, and as a metaphor for anything frozen in time.

As the Westinghouse container disappeared into the ground that Friday afternoon, an announcer proclaimed: "May the Time Capsule sleep well. When it is awakened 5,000 years from now, may its contents be found a suitable gift to our far-off descendants."

Those contents included material meant to represent "life as we live it today." There was a message from Albert Einstein, a dictionary of slang, a toothbrush, a fork and spoon, reproductions of Surrealist paintings, a Bible, a bikini, a deck of cards, and 22,000 pages of microfilm containing works of literature, popular magazines, cartoons, and encyclopedia entries on medicine, math, electricity, and dentistry.

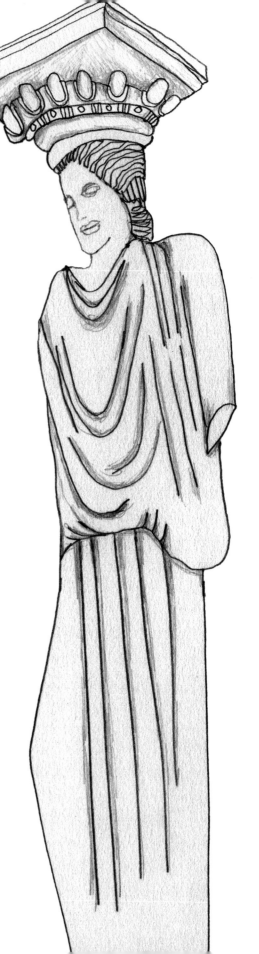

New York was chosen as the burial site because Westinghouse envisioned the city as an important future ruin. "New York will certainly be an attractive place for archaeologists 5,000 years from now, as are the sites of ancient Athens, Rome, and Troy in our own time," the company declared.

In the years since the Westinghouse project, "life as we live it today" has become a defining aspect of time capsule contents. Time capsules generally hold mundane objects, the stuff of daily life rather than the rare, costly, or extraordinary. Those things go to museums.

II. Century Boxes and Memory Chests

Prior to 1938, time capsules were known by other names. The practice of sealing a container with mementos into the foundation of a building dates back at least to ancient Assyria. These have been variously called century boxes, memory chests, and cornerstone deposits.

Seemingly every major government building in Washington, DC, holds a cornerstone deposit, usually a metal box filled with coins, newspapers, and miscellaneous civic documents. The Supreme Court, the Capitol, the Washington Monument, and the Jefferson Memorial are just a few of the DC buildings with cornerstone deposits. The White House lawns, floorboards, and walls are studded with both official and unofficial time capsules—some placed with great fanfare by presidents and first ladies, others surreptitiously stashed away by staffers or laborers working on renovations or repairs.

During the uprising for racial justice in the summer of 2020, numerous Confederate monuments were torn down. From the rubble of toppled statues, chests filled with relics emerged. There were piles of deteriorating Confederate money, Civil War bullets, and buttons ripped from military uniforms. Inside the base of the dismantled Confederate Soldiers Monument in Raleigh, North Carolina, conservators found a copper box with waterlogged contents mostly turned to sludge, though they were able to extract what was believed to be a hair from the tail of General Robert E. Lee's horse.

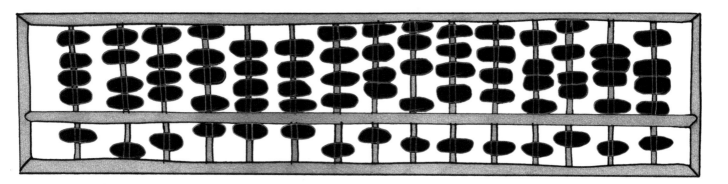

III. Big Time Capsules and Big Questions

Time capsules have been created by elementary schools and universities, by hospitals and zoos, by churches, synagogues, and mosques, by sports teams and scouting troops. There are time capsules on every continent. A nineteenth-century time capsule was discovered during preparations for the 2016 Olympics in Rio de Janeiro, Brazil. A time capsule kept near a castle in Osaka, Japan, includes an artificial eye, an abacus, a rock from Mount Everest, and utensils for a tea ceremony. In 2020, Don Victor Mooney, the first person to pilot a rowboat alone across the Atlantic Ocean, delivered to Equatorial Guinea a time capsule containing artifacts commemorating 400 years of African American history.

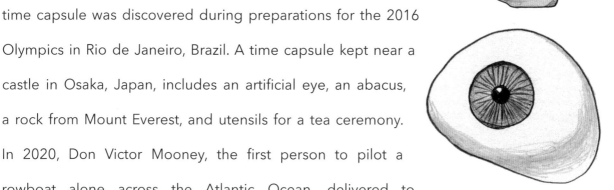

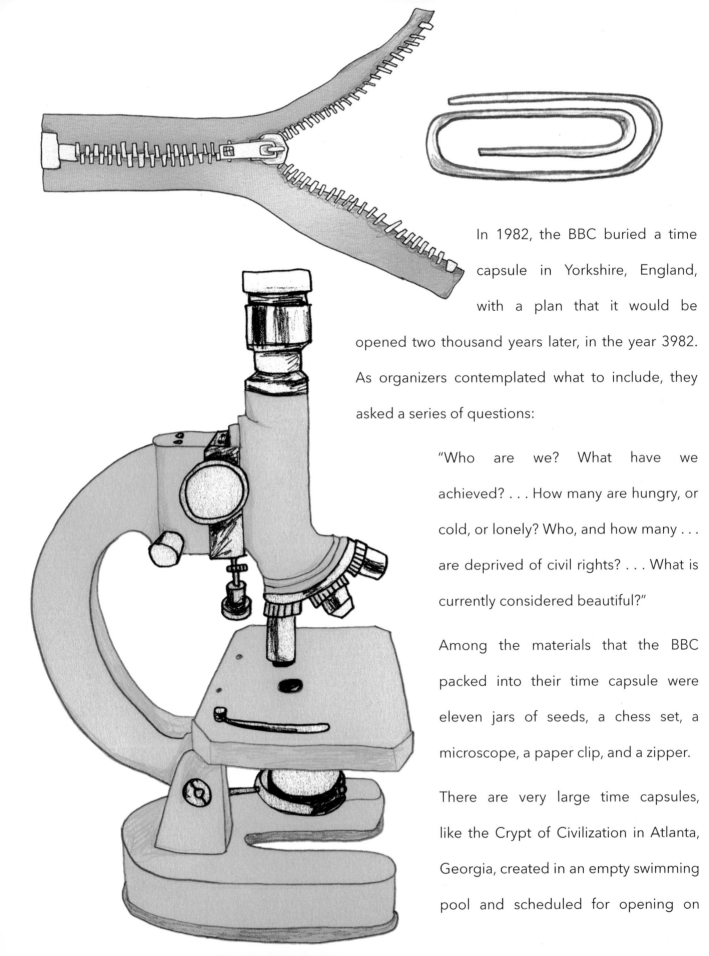

In 1982, the BBC buried a time capsule in Yorkshire, England, with a plan that it would be opened two thousand years later, in the year 3982. As organizers contemplated what to include, they asked a series of questions:

"Who are we? What have we achieved? . . . How many are hungry, or cold, or lonely? Who, and how many . . . are deprived of civil rights? . . . What is currently considered beautiful?"

Among the materials that the BBC packed into their time capsule were eleven jars of seeds, a chess set, a microscope, a paper clip, and a zipper.

There are very large time capsules, like the Crypt of Civilization in Atlanta, Georgia, created in an empty swimming pool and scheduled for opening on

May 28, 8113. A time capsule built inside an abandoned gold mine, the Tropico Time Tunnel in Rosamond, California, is jammed with home appliances.

A salt mine in Hallstatt, Austria, is the home of the Memory of Mankind time capsule, which aims to preserve human knowledge on laser-engraved disks inspired by ancient clay tablets. The project's founder worried that too much of our current existence resides only in the digital "cloud" and is vulnerable to an array of catastrophic events, from global warming to nuclear war to the simple tap of a computer's "delete" button. A sign on the wall of the mine reads: "This physical and analogue backup of our age stored here in the salt mine of Hallstatt will persist throughout all of time." Anyone is invited to submit whatever they wish to the archive.

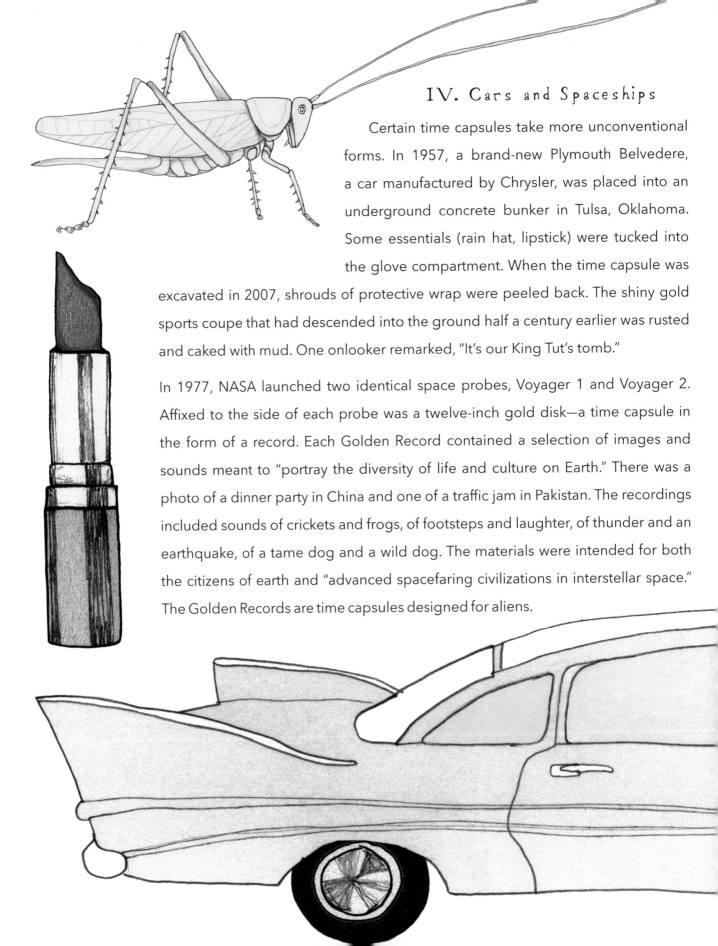

IV. Cars and Spaceships

Certain time capsules take more unconventional forms. In 1957, a brand-new Plymouth Belvedere, a car manufactured by Chrysler, was placed into an underground concrete bunker in Tulsa, Oklahoma. Some essentials (rain hat, lipstick) were tucked into the glove compartment. When the time capsule was excavated in 2007, shrouds of protective wrap were peeled back. The shiny gold sports coupe that had descended into the ground half a century earlier was rusted and caked with mud. One onlooker remarked, "It's our King Tut's tomb."

In 1977, NASA launched two identical space probes, Voyager 1 and Voyager 2. Affixed to the side of each probe was a twelve-inch gold disk—a time capsule in the form of a record. Each Golden Record contained a selection of images and sounds meant to "portray the diversity of life and culture on Earth." There was a photo of a dinner party in China and one of a traffic jam in Pakistan. The recordings included sounds of crickets and frogs, of footsteps and laughter, of thunder and an earthquake, of a tame dog and a wild dog. The materials were intended for both the citizens of earth and "advanced spacefaring civilizations in interstellar space." The Golden Records are time capsules designed for aliens.

V. Frozen in Time

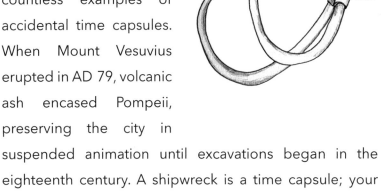

History has recorded countless examples of accidental time capsules. When Mount Vesuvius erupted in AD 79, volcanic ash encased Pompeii, preserving the city in suspended animation until excavations began in the eighteenth century. A shipwreck is a time capsule; your leftovers in the freezer are a time capsule. As climatic warming thaws arctic permafrost, long-hidden creatures surface—woolly mammoths, cave lions, the ancient relatives of rhinos, wolves, and horses. The Ice Age is a time capsule.

The time capsules that are deliberately created by human beings have been referred to as "reverse archaeology." Rather than waiting millennia for scholars to dig up our lives and make sense of smartphones, car keys, Legos, and Velcro, anyone with an airtight container and a few keepsakes can decide how they wish to be remembered and what message they want to send to the future. According to historian Nick Yablon, time capsules allow for a "radical expansion of what could count as history."

I hope this book encourages you to think like a historian, reflecting on the moment in which you live and how that moment might look five years, ten years, or five thousand years from now. I hope it helps you to think like a scientist, collecting evidence and considering the chemistry of preservation. I hope it inspires you to make art, creating three-dimensional self-portraits in words and objects.

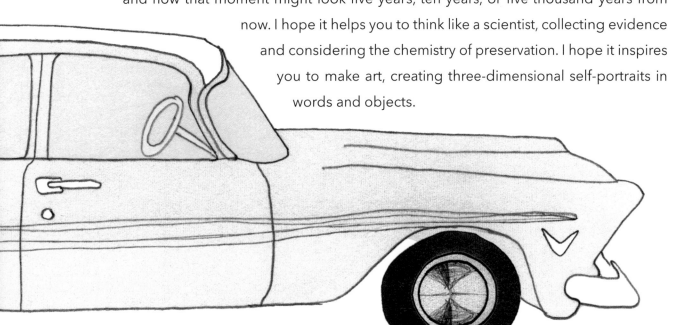

ACTIVITIES FOR FUTURIANS:
MAKE A TIME CAPSULE

Find a container that closes tightly.

Write the date inside the container.

Imagine someone from the future finding your time capsule. What do you want that person to know about you? Identify five or more objects that could help someone understand you. Draw a picture of any object that won't fit in the jar.

Write a letter to the finder of your time capsule. Some ideas to consider for your letter:

- Describe your typical day.

- Tell a funny story.

- Describe your family.

- Describe the modes of transportation you use.

- What is a challenge you faced recently?

- What technologies do you use to communicate with friends and relatives?

- Enclose a ticket stub from a trip, near or far.

- Draw a picture of someone who is important to you.

- Draw a picture of something you find beautiful. Draw a picture of something you think a person in 100 years will find beautiful.

- Include three predictions about life in 100 years.

Place your drawings, writings, and objects in the container. Seal the container and find a safe place to store it.

SELECTED BIBLIOGRAPHY

The Book of Record of the Time Capsule of Cupaloy. New York: Westinghouse Electric & Manufacturing Company, 1938.

Durrans, Brian. "Time Capsules as Extreme Collecting," in *Extreme Collecting: Challenging Practices for 21st Century Museums*. Oxford: Berghahn Books, 2014.

Jarvis, William, E. *Time Capsules: A Cultural History*. Jefferson, North Carolina: MacFarland & Company, Inc., 2002.

Moncrieff, Anthony. *Messages to the Future: The Story of the BBC Time Capsule*. London: Futura, 1984.

Sagan, Carl. *Murmurs of Earth: The Voyager Interstellar Record*. New York: Ballantine Books, 1978.

Yablon, Nick. *Remembrance of Things Present: The Invention of the Time Capsule*. Chicago: University of Chicago Press, 2019.

Many thanks to Christopher Myers, Michelle Frey, Nicole de las Heras, Elyse Cheney, Claire Gillespie, Derrick Alderman, David Ferriero, Anne Lester, Rick & Robin Redniss, and Jody Rosen. Extra special thanks to Theo Rosen for being a great hand model and for creating the time capsule jar label.

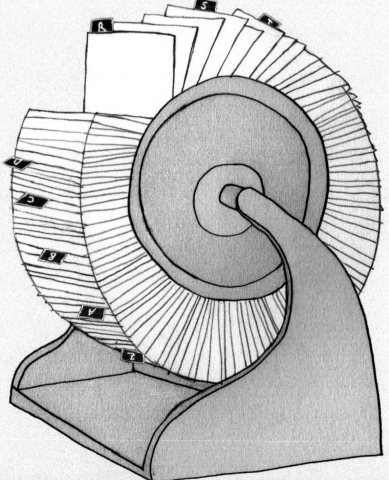

MAKE ME A WORLD

Dear Reader,

You live in momentous times. The events of the last few years will certainly be recorded in history books, will be debated in social studies classes, will be memorized as series of facts by students many years from now. If you are a child today, you will one day have a niece or a nephew, or a great-grandchild, who will ask you what it was like to live through all the things you have lived through. You will be the living link between tomorrow and today.

How you remember it all will be important.

This is a big part of what writers and artists and historians do.

We remember things. We remember them well, and vividly, and save them for later.

Lauren Redniss is a writer, journalist, artist, and thinker. She thinks a lot about memory and how we remember. She once planned a book of interviews with 100 people who were over 100 years old, and wanted to call it *10,000 Years*. She once spent a whole week in a famous museum, interviewing guards, cleaning crews, and curators, looking at what kinds of new memories are built in the places where we hold our memories. She remembers things like the lives of brilliant scientists with radioactive journals, and all the people who make one evening of ballet possible. For any big moment, there are 10,000 ways to remember it, and Lauren thinks about them all. She is an expert on how to remember.

Lauren made the book you're holding. It is a beginner's guide on how to remember. How to save the important things, and decide which are the important things for you, for your communities, for the stories that you want to tell.

You live in momentous times. These times will be over soon enough, making way for more momentous times, and all that you will have left are your memories. What will you save? What will you give to tomorrow?

Christopher Myers